World of R

Disney Junior

MARVEL

SPIDEY and his AMAZING FRIENDS

The Hangout Headache

Adapted by **Steve Behling**
Based on the episode written by **Mike Kubat**
Designed by **David Roe**

MARVEL
Los Angeles • New York

Oh, no! Green Goblin!
He is at Jerry's Junkyard.

Jerry is Hulk's friend.
The heroes will stop Goblin.

Hulk chases Goblin.
Goblin hides.

Where is Goblin?
The heroes look.

There he is! Oh, no!

Goblin wants the magnet.

Goblin is gone.
He made a mess.

Time to clean up.
Jerry uses the magnet.

"To WEB-Quarters!"
says Spidey.

"Jump down!" says Spidey.

Hulk jumps. He is too big.
Spidey goes up.

Hulk is sorry. It is okay!

Goblin wants the magnet.
Goblin takes the magnet!

Goblin uses the magnet . . .
. . . to take more!

“Drop it!” Hulk says.

Everything drops.
The heroes catch everything.

Goblin flies.
Spidey thwips.

Spidey misses.
Goblin is too high.

Hulk has a plan.
Spidey steps on.

Hulk jumps.
Spidey goes up!

Spidey has a plan.

He uses the magnet . . .

. . . to bring Goblin down.
Goblin falls.

He crashes.

Hulk gets him!

Go, Hulk! Go, Spidey!